OFF WE GO...

The Dublin Adventure

'Why do yous talk funny?' asked Michelle.
'We don't talk funny,' said Sinéad, 'you do.'

For country children, learning the ways of the big city can be a great thrill. Here Sinéad and Dara are in the city for the first time, visiting their cousin Michelle.

There are all sorts of interesting things to learn about city life and exciting places to explore. The children take to it with gusto, asking millions of questions and getting into a spot of trouble now and then.

This is a child's view of the big city.

For Clodagh, Sarah and Darragh

OFF WE GO...

The DUBLIN Adventure

Siobhán Parkinson

Illustrated by
Cathy Henderson

THE O'BRIEN PRESS
DUBLIN

First published 1992 by The O'Brien Press Ltd.,
20 Victoria Road, Dublin 6, Ireland

10 9 8 7 6 5 4 3 2 1

British Library Cataloguing-in-publication Data
A catalogue record for this book is available
from the British Library.

ISBN 0-86278-288-0

Cover design and illustration: Cathy Henderson
Typesetting, layout and design: The O'Brien Press
Printing: The Guernsey Press Co. Ltd., Channel Islands

ONE

In which we meet our hero and heroine
and the adventure starts

Sinéad and Dara live in Inishbeg, near Athenry in County Galway.

(If you've never heard of Inishbeg, that's because the people who make up the geography books left it out, so only Inishbeg people and their friends and relations know about it!)

One summer's morning, Sinéad and Dara were trying to wriggle their way into their parents' bed in their house in Inishbeg. Their mother and father were doing their best, as usual, to keep the duvet for themselves, which is just like grown-ups.

Their father opened one eye and squinted at his children and said with a sigh, 'I'm as tired as a hammer.'

Dara looked at Sinéad, and Sinéad looked at Dara.

'Is a hammer tired?' Dara asked his big sister.

'Of course it is,' said Sinéad, who always had an answer for her little brother. 'Did you ever see a hammer moving? Well, that's because it's so tired. It's too tired to move.'

'Oh,' said Dara.

'What's all this about hammers?' said their mother. 'Come on, you two, time to get dressed. This is the day you're going to Dublin.'

'Dublin?' said Sinéad

'Are we going to stay the night?' Dara asked.

'You're going to stay for a few nights,' said his mother. 'Don't you remember? At the beginning of the summer I promised you a special holiday. Well, this is it.'

'What sort of a place is Dublin?' asked Dara, as he struggled into his jumper.

'It's just a place,' said Sinéad. 'It's a bit like Galway, only more so.'

'With a Lydon's?' asked Dara hopefully.

'Well,' said Sinéad (for to tell the truth, she wasn't so sure if there was a Lydon's or not), 'well, it has a McDonald's.'

'A McDonald's?' said Dara.
'With coffee-and-walnut cakes?'

But Sinéad didn't get a chance to answer, for
before they knew it, their mother had them
scrubbed and brushed and delivered to Uncle
Dan, who was to take them to Dublin.

'Now,' said the children's mother, 'I've
packed your rucksacks. I've put
in your Mr Men toothbrush,
Dara, and Bartholomew is there
too.'

Bartholomew is a very dirty ragdoll with freckles. He is Dara's best friend.

'Are we going to stay in a hotel?' asked Sinéad. Sinéad likes hotels, because they smell of chips. Sinéad thinks that is a very promising smell.

'A hotel!' said Uncle Dan. 'Do you think we're made of money? No. We're staying with your Aunty May.'

Well, that didn't sound as good as a hotel, because the chips you get in people's houses are never as nice as the chips you get in hotels. Still, it might be interesting enough in its own way. The children thought they would wait and see.

'Has Aunty May any children?' asked Sinéad, when they were settled in the train and tucking into Coke and crisps.

'Well, she had,' said Uncle Dan.

'She *had*,' said Dara in a worried voice. 'What happened to them?'

'They grew up,' explained Uncle Dan.

'Is that all?' said Dara, relieved.

'Isn't that bad enough?' said Uncle Dan. 'Anyway,' he went on, 'her grown-up daughter lives with her. Her name is Kathleen. She'd be your Aunty Kathleen, I suppose.'

'I didn't know an aunt could have another aunt for a daughter,' said Sinéad.

'Well, she's not exactly your aunt. But she's too old for you to call her plain Kathleen.'

'I wouldn't call anyone Plain Kathleen, no matter how old they were,' said Sinéad, and the two children giggled.

'And then,' continued Uncle Dan, ignoring them, 'your Aunty Kathleen has a daughter too.'

'And is she another aunt?' asked Sinéad.

'Oh no. I suppose she's a sort of a cousin. Now, I have to read my paper, so I don't want any more ould guff out of you two.'

And Uncle Dan opened up the paper and disappeared behind it and the children looked out the window.

When the train went through towns, you could see people's back yards with their washing hanging out and dead cars up on

blocks and children mixing mud in buckets, just like they did in Inishbeg. And in the countryside all you could see were fields and more fields.

But then, after miles and miles, and long after the children had finished their Coke and crisps and had played fifteen thousand games of I Spy, there were suddenly no fields at all, just lots and lots of back gardens, and the next thing was they were clanking into Heuston Station, or Kingsbridge as Uncle Dan called it.

When they got off the train, the children put their rucksacks on their backs and they set off over the bridge and up the hill after their Uncle Dan.

Uncle Dan didn't have a rucksack or even a suitcase. He just had a brown paper bag with

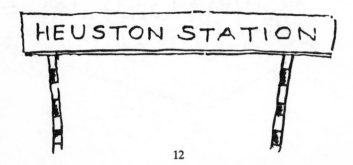

his pyjamas in it, and his newspaper rolled up under his arm.

There was an awful lot of noise in Dublin, and to tell the truth, it didn't smell very nice.

There were millions of big green double-decker buses, all coughing and rumbling away, the river was very mucky, the seagulls made a fierce racket and there were cars all over the place, swooshing around bends and hooting and tooting and being too big for their boots.

Aunty May lived in Viking Street, which was called after the Vikings, who started Dublin, as Aunty May told them.

The houses in Viking Street were all stuck together and they were all exactly the same, except that the doors were painted in different colours.

You couldn't come in the back door, unless you were only coming from the yard, and you even had to bring your bicycle in the front door, if you had a bicycle.

Sinéad and Dara saw somebody taking his motor-bike in the hall door!

It was all very different from the bungalow at home in Inishbeg.

There were stairs in Aunty May's house, that started in the kitchen and ended on a little small square of a landing.

14

Sinéad and Dara were going to sleep in Michelle's room. (Michelle was the sort-of-a-cousin.) The girls were going to share the bunk beds and Dara was going to have a camp bed.

It was pretty exciting to sleep in a camp bed or on the top bunk, but Uncle Dan was going to sleep on the sofa

downstairs, and Sinéad and Dara thought that was even more exciting.

The first thing Dara unpacked was Bartholomew.

'Is that your doll?' asked Michelle.

'Yes,' said Dara proudly.

'Boys don't play with dolls,' said Michelle.

'Of course they do,' said Sinéad. 'Dara plays with Bartholomew, and *he's* a boy.'

'Oh,' said Michelle. She couldn't think of an answer to that one.

After a while, she said: 'Why do yous talk funny?'

'*We* don't talk funny,' said Sinéad. '*You* do.'

'Oh,' said Michelle again.

And I don't think she could think of an answer to that one either!

TWO

In which the children go to town
and somebody gets lost

After lunch, Aunty Kathleen asked the children if they would like to go to town.

'But this *is* a town. It's a city, even,' said Sinéad.

'Yeh, but it's not *town*. You go *into* town, on a bus,' explained Michelle.

'A bus! That's great!' said Dara. 'Is your car in the garage?'

'We haven't got a car,' said Aunty Kathleen. 'You don't need a car in Dublin. You can go on the bus.'

Uncle Dan wasn't coming with them. He had important business to do, he said, and he would see them later.

So the three children set off for town with Aunty Kathleen.

It was a double-decker bus and the children sat upstairs.

It was a bit wobbly up there so high and sometimes branches of trees knocked on the roof over the children's heads and they got hurled about on their seats when the bus swung around corners, but Sinéad and Dara didn't mind, because they had such a good view.

They could see cars and people and shops and dogs. The people and the dogs seemed a long way down.

And they could see the roofs of the
bus-shelters, and the top parts of lamp-posts
and even the bulbs if they stretched their necks,
and they could look right down
at people's umbrellas.

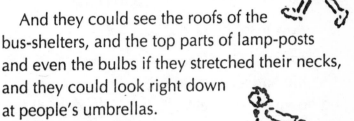

Umbrellas look completely
different if you look down at
them from up above, and the
best place to do this is from the top deck of a
bus.

When they arrived in town the children and
Aunty Kathleen went into a big
shop, because Aunty Kathleen had
some shopping to do.

19

There was a nice smell of new things in the shop and lots of people with frowns on their faces wondering what to buy and queuing up to pay for things, and there were lifts and stairs and, best of all, a moving staircase called an escalator, as Sinéad explained to Dara.

'I *know* that,' he said.

Sinéad and Dara and Michelle had a few goes up and down the escalators while Aunty Kathleen was trying on a dress in a little cubicle.

Then Michelle had a brilliant idea. 'Let's try going *up* the *down* escalator!' she cried.

So Sinéad and Michelle had a terrific time scrambling up the down escalator.

But Dara didn't like that game, because even if he ran his fastest he still only stayed in the same place.

So instead he went off down another escalator.

This was much more enjoyable really because you could just stand there and sort of sail along with your hand chasing along the moving rail beside you.

When he got to the bottom Dara took a deep breath and did a little skip, and there he was on land again.

He looked around, and he thought he must be in the North Pole where Santa lives, or in Tír na nÓg maybe, because everywhere he looked, all he could see were toys and toys and more toys.

There were rows and rows of bikes and tractors and pedal-cars.

Dara had a go on a few of these – well, not the bikes actually, because he can only *nearly* ride a bike, but he found plenty of other things that are much easier to balance on.

When he got tired pedalling around he spotted a little kitchen that was big enough to stand in and had little pots and pans and even a little sink with taps you could turn.

So he had a go at that and made a few stews and cakes and things.

And when he got tired of cooking he found a lovely little castle, with a drawbridge and knights in armour and a portcullis and all, so he had a game of Robin Hood with that.

Well, Dara had a smashing time, trying all the different toys.

As soon as he got tired of one game, he quickly found something else to play with.

He was busy drawing a monsters' house on a blackboard when he heard a loud crackly voice booming through the air.

At first he thought it must be a boy-eating giant or Aladdin's genie or some sort of a nasty from fairyland because he knew that if you found yourself in an enchanted place like this there was sure to be an ogre or a witch around – remember what happened to Hansel and Gretel when they found the gingerbread house, and to Jack when he climbed the beanstalk?

But the voice wasn't saying Fee-fi-fo-fum. It was saying:

> 'A little boy is lost.
> A little boy is lost.
> He is five years old and has curly hair.
> If you find him, please bring him to reception.'

What's 'reception'? Dara wondered. He had

an idea it had something to do with weddings.

He shrugged his shoulders, thinking to himself: Silly fellow, getting lost – probably some Dublin kid, and he got back to colouring in the blood-bottles on the doorstep of his monsters' house. (These monsters drank blood instead of milk.)

Just as he was drawing a visible hat on Mr Invisible's invisible head (which is quite hard to do, because it is very easy to forget where the head is), Dara heard the sound of running footsteps and then:

'Oh Dara, Dara, *there* you are!'

And with that Sinéad and Michelle came thundering towards him followed by Aunty Kathleen with her coat flapping open and tottering a bit in her best shoes and, bringing up the rear, a policeman.

Sinéad reached him first and threw her arms around him, and began hugging and kissing him like mad and sniffling and crying at the same time.

When Dara managed to get his face free he said: 'Hi. This is a great shop, Aunty Kathleen. Why have you got a guard with you?'

'He's not a guard,' said Sinéad, 'he's a security man.'

'Is that a two-way radio?' Dara asked the guard.

'He found your sister and your cousin being very bold on the escalators,' said Aunty Kathleen, 'and then we discovered that you were lost.'

'No, no,' explained Dara, 'that wasn't me that was lost. That was some Dublin kid.'

'We weren't being bold,' said Sinéad at the same time, starting to cry again.

'All right, all right,' said Aunty Kathleen. 'Don't cry, Sinéad. I know you didn't realise it was dangerous to play on the escalators. But Michelle should have known better.'

Before Michelle could open her mouth, Dara said: 'Why did you think I was lost? I was here all the time.'

'But we didn't know where you were,' said Aunty Kathleen. 'So you were lost.'

'But *I* knew where I was,' said Dara, 'so I *couldn't* have been lost.'

27

'You're a bit mixed up, Dara,' said Aunty Kathleen.

Dara thought to himself that it was really Aunty Kathleen who was confused, mixing him up with that other boy, but he said kindly: 'Well, I didn't know where *ye* were. So maybe it was ye who were lost.'

'Oh well, maybe so,' agreed Aunty Kathleen.

'Kids!' said the security man and shrugged his shoulders.

But then, as if to show he wasn't really cross with them, he produced a bag of sweets and offered everyone a fruit jelly.

'We're not allowed to take sweets from strangers,' said Sinéad.

'Quite right too,' said the security man. 'Especially if he's dressed up like a guard. So now what will we do?'

And the children all gazed sadly at the uneaten fruit jellies.

'Maybe we're allowed to talk to strangers if Aunty Kathleen is there to mind us,' suggested Dara.

'That's right,' said Aunty Kathleen. 'The very thing!' And she popped a juicy blackberry sweet into her mouth.

After that, they left the shop and went to have a look at a little waterfall in the middle of O'Connell Street with a big green woman lying under it. It's a funny sort of a thing to have in the middle of the street, but the children liked it because you can wiggle your fingers in the water.

'She's getting very wet,' said Dara. 'Is she a mermaid?'

'No,' said Aunty Kathleen. 'She's called Anna Livia. She's more a sort of a river queen. River queens aren't supposed to mind getting wet.'

'Neither do mermaids,' said Dara.

'It looks more like a bath than a river,' said Sinéad.

'No it doesn't,' said Michelle. 'Baths are more roundy.'

'It's a fountain,' said Aunty Kathleen firmly, and herded the children across the road and up a busy street.

'Now we'll go and have something nice,' she said, 'and then we'll have to go home.'

'Something nice to *eat*?' asked Dara. 'In Lydon's? Or McDonald's?'

'No. In Bewley's. You can eat in McDonald's in any old city, but you can only eat in Bewley's in Dublin.'

'Well, there's a Bewley's in Galway now,' said Sinéad.

'But it's not the same,' said Aunty Kathleen. 'This is a special Bewley's with a lovely stained glass window.'

Sinéad and Dara thought stained glass didn't sound very nice, but Bewley's did, and they all suddenly felt very hungry.

There was a lot of clatter in Bewley's and a lovely rich, warm, sweet smell. Aunty Kathleen said that was the smell of coffee beans roasting.

'Do you eat them hot?' Dara asked.

'No,' said Michelle, 'you make coffee out of them, if you like coffee. I don't, but I like the smell.'

The Inishbeg children didn't like coffee either but they loved the milk and sticky buns that Aunty Kathleen very kindly bought them.

And they liked the special window too. The glass wasn't stained at all (perhaps the window cleaners had been there since Aunty Kathleen was last in Bewley's). It was all lovely colours, which made wavery blue and red shapes on the tables, and the bits of coloured glass made a picture a bit like a big glass jigsaw.

'We're sorry for being bold,' said Sinéad, when they were sitting down.

'And for losing you,' said Dara.

'Oh, you're not too bad,' said Aunty Kathleen. 'For country kids!'

Michelle looked a bit put out at this.

'You're not too bad either,' her mother told her. 'But then, you're a real jackeen!'

THREE

In which the children go on
a short expedition

Sometimes, when they weren't too busy playing, the children went with Aunty May down Manor Street and Stoneybatter to get the meat for the dinner and on down to Smithfield to get fruit and vegetables at the market.

One day, when they were coming back from Portobello, where Aunty May's

ST. PATRICK'S

CHRIST CHURCH

sister lives, they saw St Patrick's Cathedral, which is tall and old, and Christ Church Cathedral, which is fat and old.

Aunty May told the children that Strongbow's tomb was in Christ Church.

Of course Sinéad knew all about Strongbow and she told Michelle and Dara the whole story. Dara hadn't heard it before because he is too young to do history, and Michelle didn't know it because she doesn't listen in class.

The next day, Aunty Kathleen said they were going on an outing.

'What's an outing?' asked Dara.

'It's like an expedition,' said Aunty Kathleen, 'only shorter.'

'Oh,' said Dara, but he thought that wasn't a very helpful explanation.

'We're going to the National Gallery and to the Natural History Museum,' said Aunty Kathleen.

'Not the Natural History Museum!' exclaimed Michelle. 'It'll be all bones and stones.'

'You're talking through your hat, Michelle,' said Aunty Kathleen. 'And anyway, I bet Sinéad and Dara will like it.'

'But I'm too small for history,' said Dara.

'Not for this kind of history, Dara,' said Aunty Kathleen.

The first thing they saw when they got to the museum was a huge animal skeleton high up on a stand.

'Is that an animal from giant-land?' asked Dara.

'Sort of,' said Aunty Kathleen. 'It's a skeleton of a giant deer. There used to be lots of them in Ireland long ago, but they've all died out.'

'Is it a sort of a dinosaur?' asked Dara.

'No, it's not as old as a dinosaur,' said Aunty Kathleen, 'but it looks nearly as big.'

'Wow!' said Sinéad and Dara. Even Michelle looked interested.

'I hope its ghost isn't around,' whispered Dara.

'Deer don't have ghosts,' said Sinéad.

'I bet they have,' said Michelle.

'These other animals look real,' said Dara, pointing to a glass case where a fox was holding a dead bird in its mouth and some rabbits were sitting outside their burrow.

'They *are* real,' said Aunty Kathleen.

'Oh!' said Dara, jumping back from the case.

'But they're dead,' explained his aunt.
'They can't be,' said Dara. 'They're standing up.'

'They're stuffed, silly,' said Sinéad.

'Oh,' said Dara. 'Have they been to a party?'

'Not stuffed with food, Dara,' said Aunty Kathleen. 'They have been specially stuffed to keep them looking nice and alive. The museum people have put them standing up to show you how they would have looked when they were living animals.'

Sinéad and Michelle went from case to case looking at the animals and birds and reading the little cards that told you what all the creatures were.

But Dara stood well back from the cases and looked from a safe distance.

Well, you never know, do you?

After that, they walked down the street to the National Gallery. They went into a long high room, with a double staircase.

'Hey, cool,' said Michelle. 'Like in *Gone with the Wind*.'

Dara stared up at a big white statue.

'Is that person real, or is he stuffed or dead or what?' asked Dara.

'It's not a person. It's a sculpture,' said Aunty Kathleen. 'It's a bit like a picture, except that it's carved out of marble instead of just being painted flat.'

'Oh, I see,' said Dara, still staring up at the big white person. 'Who is it a carving of?'

'Oh, I don't know. Somebody from Ancient Greece I think,' said Aunty Kathleen.

'Was Ancient Greece a very long time ago?' asked Dara.

'Yes,' said Aunty Kathleen. 'Thousands of years ago.'

'I thought so,' said Dara. 'Because it must have been before they invented clothes.' He went on, 'You'd think they'd have had fur, in those days.'

'Maybe the artist thought he looked nicer that way,' suggested Aunty Kathleen.

'But he must have been very cold,' said Dara. Which is quite true, and probably explains why he was so pale.

After the statue, they looked at some of the pictures.

There was a huge one, which nearly filled a whole wall, showing Strongbow's wedding to the princess Aoife.

'That's the fellow whose tomb is in the fat old church, isn't it?' said Dara.

'I thought you said you were too small for history, Dara,' said Aunty Kathleen. 'You're quite right, though. He is buried in Christ Church Cathedral.'

Dara got quite pink and put on a pleased sort of grin.

Sinéad's favourite picture was of a girl with a flock of geese in a field of blue flowers.

Dara's favourite was of a racehorse. At least, he said it was a racehorse, but Sinéad said it was just a messy picture.

Michelle's favourite was of a man in old-fashioned clothes with a sword and a cape and long white stockings and bows on his shoes.

Aunty Kathleen said she liked so many of the pictures that she couldn't choose a favourite.

And then, because the children had been really good in the museum and the gallery, Aunty Kathleen took them up to St Stephen's Green to play in the adventure playground.

It's a great playground, with lovely wooden battlements for climbing on and rope ladders and things, and a tunnel to crawl through, as well as the ordinary toys like swings and see-saws.

42

When they were tired of the playground, they went to see the ducks on the pond, but they only fed them a few crumbs, because Sinéad had read in a book that sliced pan is not the best diet for ducks and they couldn't find any frogs or slugs or things to feed them instead.

Coming out of the Green, at the top of Grafton Street, they saw a very strange-looking gent with his hair all shaved off and his face painted and wearing funny clothes.

He was taking long slow steps, and his eyes were popping at people.

'It's an ostrich,' said Dara.

'It's a clown,' said Sinéad.

'No, he's just an actor. He's an ad for something,' explained Michelle. 'He's called the Diceman.'

'He doesn't look much like a dice to me,' sniffed Sinéad.

'He doesn't even look much like a man,' said Michelle.

The Diceman stopped his long, slow steps and popped his eyes at Michelle.

They all hurried along down the street after that.

Michelle looked back over her shoulder once and the funny ostrich-clown-man seemed still to be popping his eyes. She hoped it wasn't at her!

FOUR

In which Bartholomew has a birthday and the children
make a phone-call home

All the Viking Street children played on the street, because they didn't have any gardens. They brought their toys out onto their doorsteps and played on the footpath.

One day Dara decided to have a birthday party for Bartholomew on the street.

Bartholomew must be about a hundred by now, because he is always having birthdays, but since he is a doll it doesn't show.

Michelle's friend Tracy, who lives across the street, has lots of dolls and teddies, whom Bartholomew very kindly invited to his party even though he didn't know them very well.

A boy called Brendan from the other end of the street came along with his toy dog and asked if he could go to the party too, and Bartholomew said yes he could if he didn't mind sharing a plate with Tracy's panda.

They were planning to have pretend food only as it was a dolls' party after all.

But when Aunty May heard about it she arrived out with jam sandwiches with the crusts cut off and a big jug of Ribena, so the children let the dolls have all the pretend food and they shared the jam sandwiches and the Ribena.

The children enjoyed playing in Viking Street, but they liked it even better when they went places.

When Aunty Kathleen was at work and
Aunty May was busy at other things, the
children sometimes went for walks with Uncle
Dan.

He showed them the new houses where the
big Dublin Cattle Market used to be.

Uncle Dan used to come to Dublin to sell
cattle when he was a young man and he would
stay with Aunty May in those days too. Aunty
Kathleen could remember that from when she
was a girl.

Michelle couldn't believe there had ever
been cattle in Dublin.

'Didn't they make a terrible mess?' she asked.
'Oh they did, they did,' agreed Uncle Dan.
'A terrible mess entirely. But you know, a
cow-pat is clean dirt.'

'Well, what's dirty dirt, then?' asked Michelle.

'Oh,' said Uncle Dan, 'really dirty dirt is made by cars and buses and lorries and factories and people, not by grass-eating animals.'

'Well, I wouldn't like to step on any of that clean dirt all the same, thank you very much,' said Michelle.

One day Uncle Dan took them to the Phoenix Park and they saw the deer in the distance and the Furry Glen and Mrs Robinson's big white house.

Uncle Dan told them that not very long ago farmers used to graze their cattle in the Phoenix Park, but now the only big animals in the park are the deer.

'That's not true,' said Michelle. 'What about all the animals in the zoo?'

'Oh, that's right,' said Uncle Dan, 'I was

forgetting them. Let's go and have a peek at them, will we?'

The children didn't have any money with them that day, so they didn't visit the zoo, but they had a good squint in through the wire meshing, which was nearly as good.

They could see the ostriches and the rhino and they heard the sea-lions hooting out to their keepers because it was feeding time.

That evening, Uncle Dan said it would be a good idea to ring home to Inishbeg, to let Sinéad and Dara's parents know how they were getting on.

So off they went with Uncle Dan and Aunty Kathleen to the telephone box because Aunty May had no phone in the house.

Uncle Dan had a handful of coins and he dialled the number for the children.

Then he got out of the box because it is a bit of a squash with three people, even if two of them are small.

Sinéad spoke first to her mother and then to her father. Then it was Dara's turn.

'Hello, Daddy, Daddy, Daddy!' he shouted into the phone.

'Dad, we're having a great time. Sinéad got lost in a big shop and a guard found her, and we fed the ducks and we were in Smithfield, and Bartholomew had a birthday, and the stairs move up and down all by themselves, and we saw a man that walks like an ostrich and a woman with no clothes on in a bath in the middle of the street, and a dinosaur's skeleton.'

'Oh, I think I'd better come up to Dublin and rescue you,' said his dad. 'It all sounds very peculiar.'

'Oh no, Daddy, don't do that. Not yet,' wailed Dara. 'It's great fun and I have a camp bed and we go everywhere on the bus.'

'Beep-beep-beep-beep,' said the telephone.

'Daddy! Daddy! Where are you?' sobbed Dara. 'He's gone! He's gone!'

'It's all right, Dara, don't worry,' said Aunty Kathleen soothingly, 'he's not gone. It's just that we ran out of money, so the phone-call got cut off.'

'I'll tell you what,' she went on, because she had just had an idea that she thought might cheer Dara up. 'Tomorrow I'll take you all to see the Vikings.'

'The ones who started Dublin?' asked Dara, looking quite cheered up already.

'The very ones,' said Aunty Kathleen.

FIVE

In which the children meet the Vikings,
who started Dublin

The next day, as she had promised, Aunty Kathleen took the children off to see the Vikings.

Sinéad knew all about Vikings and long-boats and round towers and Wood Quay and everything, because of being good at history.

Michelle knew all about them too because of being a Dubliner.

Dara knew nothing at all about the Vikings

except that they started Dublin.

When they arrived at the Viking place, they had to go in a special lift that was supposed to be a time machine to take them back to Viking times.

The lift made a very exciting whirring sort of noise and stopped with a clunk that made everyone's stomach swoop, and suddenly the doors slid open and they had arrived back in the tenth century.

They were met by a hairy Viking, who started spouting off at them something about a wedding and getting ready for a feast.

'A wedding?' said Dara, pulling at Aunty Kathleen's skirt to get her attention. 'Were there Vi-queens as well?'

'What?' said Aunty Kathleen.

54

'Vi-queens,' Dara explained patiently, though he knew it was not polite of Aunty Kathleen to say What?

'I thought there were only Vi-kings,' he said. 'But if somebody is getting married that means there must be women Vi-kings too and women Vi-kings must be Vi-queens, mustn't they?'

'Oh Dara!' everyone said, and laughed.

'Well, of course there were women too,' said Sinéad. 'Otherwise there wouldn't have been any Viking children and if there were no Viking children, well the Vikings wouldn't have lasted very long, would they?'

This seemed very sensible, but Dara felt a bit hurt because everyone had laughed at him.

'Never mind,' he said to Bartholomew, 'I'm sure there were Vi-children too and Vi-dolls.'

Just then, he spotted a Vi-doll, thrown in a corner. He picked it up to introduce it to

Bartholomew, but suddenly a very dirty child who might have been a boy or who might have been a girl came tearing out of a sort of a tenty house and snatched the ragdoll out of Dara's hand and ran off with it.

They didn't seem very friendly, these Vi-people.

'Do you come from beyond the seas?' the hairy Viking was asking Aunty Kathleen.

'Well,' said Aunty Kathleen. 'Not exactly. I come from just across the river, but these children come from the West of Ireland.'

'The West of Ireland?' said the Viking, surprised. 'Beyond the Bog of Allen? Great Thor! I believe there are wild beasts and terrible monsters in the West of Ireland.'

'Oh yes,' agreed Sinéad. 'My Uncle Dan has a fierce wild sow that breaks out of her sty every now and then and goes squealing and storming around the countryside and rooting up people's potatoes.'

'Potatoes?' said the Viking in a puzzled tone.

'Oh you wouldn't have heard of those,' said Sinéad. 'They weren't invented until the seventeenth century.'

'Ah!' said the Viking.

What rubbish, thought Dara. Whoever heard of inventing a potato!

Suddenly the Viking let out a roar of terror.

'Do you come in peace or to do battle?' he cried.

'Oh in peace, in peace,' Aunty Kathleen assured him.

'Then why do you carry your sword?' shouted the Viking, pointing at Aunty Kathleen's umbrella.

'Oh, this is just for protection,' Aunty

Kathleen explained, waving the umbrella about a bit and making the Viking jump back.

'Hmmm,' said the Viking, 'I suppose you're Christian Irish, are you?'

'Most certainly we are,' said Aunty Kathleen firmly. 'But we have no gold chalices or anything like that on us, not just at the moment.'

'Oh well, all right,' said the Viking sulkily. 'I suppose you can come into our city anyway.'

Well, you should have seen what he called a city – a few poky wooden houses and a very dirty street, and it didn't seem to be very clean dirt either.

There was not a traffic light to be seen, nor a lamp-post, nor a bus, nor an office block.

It was more like a very badly kept camp-site, and it was very noisy and smelly (even noisier and smellier than Dublin is today – or at least the noises and smells were different) with children and goats and goodness knows what running around the mucky street.

The Viking took them into some of the houses to meet other Vikings.

The men were all dressed like him and one of them was hairier than the next.

The women wore long robes, some of them tied in the middle with bits of string.

The houses seemed to have lots of bits of string holding them together too, and they were low and dark inside with only one room and everything was covered in what looked a bit like dirty sheepskin rugs. They were in fact sheepskins and deerskins, and probably other sorts of skin too.

Everyone was doing very different sort of work from what most people do in Dublin today.

There were no bus-drivers or teachers or typists or factory-workers or lawyers.

Instead, the people were all making things that people use every day like bread and belts and combs and cloth.

Somebody offered the children some soup out of a pot that looked a bit like a witch's cauldron, but it didn't look very appetising so they said no thank you.

Michelle was very impressed when she found out that Viking children didn't have to go to school. She thought that meant they could play all day. I think maybe she had an idea that she might stay in Viking Dublin altogether and not bother going back to the twentieth century.

But Sinéad said she thought they probably

had to help the grown-ups with the work instead.

Michelle was just thinking that didn't sound too bad when they caught sight of a girl of about nine all bent over and lugging a very heavy-looking sack on her back.

Their Viking guide explained that the girl's mother did a lot of spinning and that the girl was bringing her some fresh wool. It looked like hard work.

In fact most things looked like hard work, as there were no machines to help, and of course all the day's work had to be done before dark as there was no electric light.

Dara thought he wouldn't much like to be in this place at night, with only the firelight flickering in the houses and no light at all on the streets, unless there was a moon.

'Did you people start Dublin?' he asked the Viking.

'That's right,' said the Viking. 'We're very good sailors, of course, and we understand how to navigate by the stars. So we set off from our homelands in Scandinavia in search of new lands, and after many weeks at sea we came to these lands of Britain and Ireland and so we settled here and founded towns.'

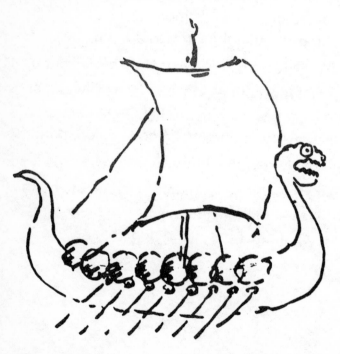

'Oh, were there towns here already? I thought it was just woods and rivers,' said Dara.

'No,' said the Viking. 'There were no towns. We settled here and built up the towns ourselves, as I said.'

'That's *not* what you said,' persisted Dara. 'You said the towns were here already.'

'No I didn't', said the Viking, getting cross now.

'Yes you did,' said Dara.

'No, I never said that,' shouted the Viking. 'We arrived here and we started Dublin. We started the city of Dublin. We founded it.'

'There you go again,' said Dara. 'First you said you started it, then you said you found it. How could you find it if it wasn't here already?'

'I TOLD YOU,' roared the Viking, who by now was getting very red in the face. 'It wasn't here.

We didn't find it. We FO ...'

Suddenly he burst out laughing.

'Oh sorry,' he said, chuckling into his beard
and putting his hand on Dara's head in that
irritating way grown-ups have, and tossing his
hair.

'I should have explained that we *found-ed* it.
To found a place means to start it up. It's not
the same as to *find* a place.'

Now it was Dara who was red in the face.

'Yeh, well,' he said, 'of course, I *knew* that.
It's just, you weren't speaking very clearly,
that's all.'

'Oh sorry, sorry, sorry,' said the Viking. 'It's
this language you speak here. I'm not very
good at it, you know. Norse is much easier.'

By now the children and Aunty Kathleen had
seen all over the tiny little settlement. Now it

was time to get back into the lift and travel forward in time again to present-day Dublin, so they said goodbye and off they went.

They blinked when they arrived back in the present.

Outside there was a nice friendly traffic jam and a jet aeroplane swooshed overhead making a comforting sort of a racket, and people were queuing for buses, and pushing prams, and dodging across the road in and out between the cars, and licking ice-cream cones, and zipping up anoraks, and using their bank cards to get money out of 'hole-in-the-wall' machines, and doing all sorts of familiar twentieth-century things.

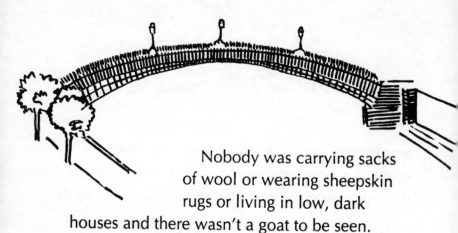

Nobody was carrying sacks of wool or wearing sheepskin rugs or living in low, dark houses and there wasn't a goat to be seen.

It was hard to believe that this busy, noisy city had started off like the Viking settlement they had just seen.

The city had tarred roads and flashing lights, whizzing DART trains and grinding traffic, tall buildings of brick and concrete and steel and glass, banks and department stores and offices, and bus-stops and railway-stations and bridges, churches and steeples and universities and schools, housing estates and blocks of flats and shopping centres, art galleries and museums and restaurants, and Molly Malone and Parnell and Big Jim Larkin and the Children of Lir, and parks and gardens and playgrounds.

And it was full of people like the tall man selling magazines outside Bewley's and the ostrich-man taking long steps and popping his eyes, and Aunty Kathleen and Michelle and Tracy and Brendan with his toy dog, and Aunty May's sister in Portobello and Mrs Robinson in the Park.

It really was hard to believe that all these things grew out of a cluster of poky little wooden buildings belonging to a baker and a comb-maker, a leather-worker and a boat-builder, a spinner and a weaver.

On the way home, they all sat on the top deck of the bus as usual.

Looking out of the window, Michelle spotted a dark-skinned, dark-haired couple, with a dark baby in a buggy. The woman was wearing a bright sari.

'Oh look!' she called. 'An Indian family!'

The others crowded around the window to see the Indian family.

'Isn't the baby lovely!' said Dara.

'Isn't the sari beautiful!' said Sinéad, who had only ever seen a sari in pictures before.

'They must be on their holidays,' said Dara.

'I don't think so,' said Aunty Kathleen. 'They probably live here. Maybe they work here and live here now all the time, or maybe they are studying here and are here for a few years.'

'Cities are like that,' she explained to the children. 'Lots of people come to a big city to work or to study or just to live for a short while and sometimes they stay and make the city their home.'

'Like the Vikings,' said Dara.

'Well, I suppose so,' smiled Aunty Kathleen. 'But more like your Aunty May, who came here from Athenry when she was a young woman and married your Uncle Jack and never went back to the country afterwards, except on holidays. And now her family have grown up and live in Dublin, and her grandchildren are all real Dubliners. That's how cities grow.'

'But it all started with the Vikings, didn't it?' said Dara. 'They found-ed Dublin, didn't they?'

'That's right,' said Aunty Kathleen, 'and people have been finding it ever since!'

SIX

*In which the children go home
and the story ends*

The very next day, Sinéad and Dara had a letter from their mother saying that school would be starting again shortly and that they needed to get their schoolbooks and get them covered and they needed to get winter shoes and runners for PE and wondering if Dara wanted to start piano this year and whether Sinéad was going to stay at ballet or would she prefer to go to Irish dancing.

Well, these are decisions not to be taken lightly and Sinéad

 thought that the best thing would be to go home and discuss them with their parents.

Dara thought this was probably the best thing too.

Michelle thought they were both daft to be thinking about school and dancing lessons and boring things when it was still only the middle of the summer.

But Sinéad explained to her that their parents were probably lonely without them.

Michelle sniffed and said see if *she* cared whether they went home and left her all by herself.

'All by yourself!' said Sinéad. 'But you live in the city, with thousands and thousands of other people.'

'Well, they're mostly grown up and anyway, I don't know them all,' argued Michelle. (Lots of people are like Michelle – when they get sad or lonely or upset they argue.) Which all goes to show that Michelle had got rather fond of her country cousins.

'I'll tell you what,' said Sinéad. 'Why don't you come to visit us in Inishbeg in the next holidays?'

'Would there be cows?' asked Michelle.

'They're all in fields,' Sinéad reassured her.

'Um,' said Michelle.

Dara began to get quite excited about going home. He started to get packed right away, and he told Bartholomew all about the train, even though Bartholomew had been on the train before and knew all about it.

The only problem was that the children didn't know whether Uncle Dan had finished all his business and was ready to come home.

Every day, he disappeared off out of the house with his newspaper folded up and tucked under his arm and every evening Aunty May asked him, 'How was business today?'

Most days he just grunted.

So that evening, Sinéad asked him if his business was finished.

'No,' said Uncle Dan. 'Fortunately not.'

'Oh,' said Sinéad. 'Does that mean we won't be going home just yet?'

'Certainly not!' said Uncle Dan. 'Do you want to go home?'

'Well,' said Sinéad. 'We have to get our winter shoes and our runners and our dancing shoes and our piano music and our copybooks and our schoolbooks and maybe even new schoolbags.'

'Good heavens!' said Uncle Dan, 'You're an expensive pair of items! And maybe,' he went on, 'maybe you're getting a bit lonely for your Ma and Da.'

'Oh no,' said Sinéad. 'Or maybe Dara is. And I think maybe they're getting lonely for us,

'Well, we can't have that,' said Uncle Dan. 'We'd better phone up CIE or whatever they call themselves nowadays and see if they have e'er a train we could take.'

'But what about your business?' asked Sinéad.

'Don't worry your head about that, girl,' said Uncle Dan. 'Sure I can do my little bit of business anywhere.'

'But I thought you came to Dublin on business,' said Sinéad.

'I did. I did. Certainly I did. Isn't it my business to take my favourite grandniece and my favourite grandnephew on holidays?'

Now Sinéad and Dara are Uncle Dan's only grandniece and grandnephew so that is not such a compliment as it appears, but it made the children feel special all the same.

'And are you sure you don't mind going home?' asked Sinéad.

'Not at all,' said Uncle Dan. 'Haven't I a farm to be getting home to anyway?'

And so arrangements were made.

The children packed their rucksacks and

they helped Aunty Kathleen to fold up the camp bed.

Uncle Dan put his pyjamas in a Superquinn bag and folded up his newspaper extra tightly.

Aunty May packed one of her famous picnics for the journey – ham sandwiches with mustard for Uncle Dan and without mustard for the children, a hard-boiled egg each, a bar of chocolate to share and a flask of tea for Uncle Dan and little packets of orange juice with straws for Sinéad and Dara.

Aunty May and Michelle went to the station with the travellers and helped them to find a nice seat on the train in a compartment with a table so they could spread out their picnic and play a game of Snap later on.

Then the Dublin people had to get off the train, because there was a piercing whistle and the train chugged a bit and groaned as if it was stretching its legs, getting ready to set off.

Sinéad and Dara and Uncle Dan pressed their noses to the window and waved at Aunty May and Michelle and suddenly, with hardly a moan, the train slid out of the station, and they were on their way.

There they go, back past the houses and gardens and washing lines and the children mixing mud in buckets (the same children, the same buckets, probably different mud), the bog-cotton fluttering in the breeze.

Away from the roar of the traffic and the aircraft, way way away from the Vikings and the time-machine and the stained glass window and roasting coffee beans in Bewley's and the over-fed ducks in Stephen's Green and the big white cold man in the National Gallery and Strongbow and Aoife and all the rest of them.

Back to the countryside, back to the low stone walls and damp little fields of East Galway.

Maybe their cousin Michelle will visit them one day as she promised.

And maybe we will meet them all again one day.

In the meantime, there they are, peeling the top layers off the sandwiches to check them for mustard and looking forward to seeing the farm again and Inishbeg and their mother and father.

And there's Uncle Dan, deep in the paper as usual and wondering whether the train will arrive in time for him to get in a bit of business before the last race.